# Goss
## CASTLE

This book belongs to

.......................................................

DEDICATION

To all the children who are starting school!

By A. Goss

Dash Dinosaur has woken up this morning and is very excited because today is a very special day.

Dash is going to school for the very first time!

Let's look at how Dash gets ready for school:

A red school cardigan with the school badge on it.

Polished scales and clipped claws.

A pencil case full of pens and pencils.

A school bag to put everything in!

"I got ready for school all by myself," smiles Dash.

Dash is ready and ROARING to go!

"Don't you look smart!" beams Daddy Dino and Mummy Dino.

"Just be yourself and you'll have a wonderful time," grins Granny Dino.

"I remember my first day at school was super duper fun!" shouts Dash's older sister, Stella.

Just as Dash and Daddy Dino begin walking to school, Dash starts to feel a **wobbly** feeling.

Dash is a bit worried about going to school for the first time.

"What if I don't make any friends?" Dash asks Daddy Dino.

"Everything will be fine," Daddy Dino smiles.

"It's normal that it feels a bit scary on your first day at school. Just remember...

Try to be **brave** and try to be **kind**, every single day,
Always try to do your **best**, that's the Dino way."

"The school looks **GINORMOUS** and there are so many dinosaurs everywhere!" thought Dash, as they arrived in the school playground.

Dash can see a whole herd of big dinosaurs. They all seem to know each other already, but there aren't any other dinosaurs who look quite like Dash.

"Have a great day," says Daddy Dino, as he blows Dash a kiss.

Behind Dash, a small dinosaur cries "Help me!" but Dash doesn't hear and waves goodbye to Daddy Dino.

Next, Dash goes inside the school and spots some other young dinosaurs that are in the same class.

Dash would quite like to make friends with some of these dinosaurs, but is also feeling a little bit shy.

"I don't know what to say to them," worries Dash.

"What if they don't like me?"

Dash decides to go straight to the cloakroom instead.

Stella
Stega

Teri
Ptero

Brandy
Brachio

Riley
Raptor

In the cloakroom, Dash encounters a **BIG** problem.

Tiny T-rex arms are too short to hang bags on pegs!

Dash is so embarrassed!

In the corner of the room, a small voice cries "Help me! Help me!" once again.

It is Riley Raptor, who is also finding it very difficult to put his bag on a peg.

A **THUD! THUD! THUD!** noise comes from behind Dash, followed by a long, tall shadow appearing over Dash's shoulder.

"Would you like some help?"

Dash turns around to see a friendly-looking Brachiosaurus.

"Y-yes please," Dash stammers nervously.

"My name is Brandy," the Brachiosaurus says as she scoops up Dash's and Riley's bags and hooks them on the pegs. "Would you like to be friends?"

"I'm Dash, and I would love to be friends!"

As they make their way into the classroom, Dash meets their new teacher.

"My name is Mister Styra" says the teacher. Dash knows that Mister Styra is short for Mister Styracosaurus. Dash feels very clever.

Mister Styra shows Dash and the other dinosaurs all the interesting things they have in the classroom.

There are books on shelves, and art on the wall.
Big rock tables and chairs for all.

The dinosaurs play roaring games to get to know each other. It is now Dash's time to roar.

At first Dash feels scared, but then Dash remembers that Daddy Dino said 'try to be brave,' so Dash tries really hard to make a big **ROAR!**

Wow! Well done, Dash!

But Dash doesn't see Riley Raptor in the corner.

Dash's roar is too loud for Riley.

It is lunchtime and Dash is sitting down with Brandy and Stella.

"This tastes great!" say the three friends as they **CRUNCH** and **MUNCH** on their school lunch.

But Riley Raptor doesn't have any lunch and is very sad indeed.

Will Dash help Riley?

"Hello," says Dash "why are you sad?"

Riley tells Dash that he can't find where to get lunch.

"I can help you," says Dash, kindly.

Dash helps Riley get lunch from the school cafeteria and they all make room at the table for Riley.

"My name is Dash! Would you like to be my friend?"

"Of course I will be your friend! My name is Riley!" says Riley Raptor.

Dash feels great for being really kind to Riley and is very happy to make another new friend on the first day of school!

At the end of the day, the school bell rings to let everyone know it is time to go home.

**DING! DING!**

Dash is so happy to see Daddy Dino.

"Did you have a good day, Dash?" says Daddy Dino

"Yes!" says Dash.

"I was brave, I was kind and I always tried my best!"

**The end**

# Dino Facts

Did you know these interesting things about dinosaurs?

1. The name 'Dinosaur' is a Greek word that means 'terrible lizard'.

2. Dinosaurs are the biggest animals that have ever lived!

3. The longest dinosaur ever was the Argentinosaurus at 37 metres tall!

4. The first dinosaurs existed 230 million years ago. Long before people walked the earth.

5. Before the dinosaurs, other living things like giant dragonflies, fish and reptiles ruled the world.

# Questions about going to school

 What did Dash do before going to school?

 How did Dash feel about going to school for the first time?

 What did Dash do at school?

 What do you think school will be like for you?

# Draw yourself on your first day of school!

Visit GossCastle.com and subscribe to the Goss Castle Newsletter for free books, activities and more!

Your reviews help us get more kids learning through reading. Please share your feedback

1.  Go to Amazon
2.  Click Orders
3.  Find the book and click Write a Product Review

Thank you

Goss
CASTLE

# Get the Dash Dinosaur series!

Printed in Great Britain
by Amazon

46239984R00021